Some Time After

Some Time After

AND OTHER POEMS

by

ANNE RIDLER

FABER AND FABER
3 Queen Square
London

First published in 1972
by Faber and Faber Limited
3 Queen Square London WC1
Printed in Great Britain by
W & J Mackay Limited, Chatham
All rights reserved

ISBN 0 571 09785 5

Contents

Acknowledgements are due to the editors of the following publications, in which some of these poems first appeared: *The Cornhill, The Critical Quarterly, The Listener, The New York Times, The Oxford Magazine, The Sunday Times, Aquarius, Four Quarters* (La Salle, Philadelphia), *Wave.*

For a New Voice

For G.

Muse of middle-age, ice on the wings,
   Earthbound looks toward skies
Where once she looped and curtsied;
   Or, hovercraft close to the ground, goes
   On a cushion of stale air,
The breath of bygone verses.
Too conscious of too much, waits
   For the irresistible moment,
   Through days, months, years, silent.

Each year a bird moults, new plumes
   For old acquires, new voice
   After the winter whisper;
And a boy before his manhood comes
   Breaks his old flute, is given
   The key of bass or tenor.

O Muse, who should be heavenly, break
   My voice, make me a new one!
Rid me of this old sound-box,
   Trap of exhausted echoes
And coffin of past power.
   Make it anew, and now:
Not swan-like, in my dying hour
   Only to sing in pain,
   But now, a poet's voice again.

A Taste for Truth

For *miracle*, they say, translate *a sign*.
If God made water into wine
What was his meaning? That his laws
Are not immutable? Though our state is miserable
Yet all might live in glory if they chose?
Wine of our joy and water of our tears
Are not so incompatible as we think
If the atoms did not change, but those who drank.

    In salt water our life began
    And our blood is a salt solution.
    We live upon this one condition—
    Salt is good, salt is bitter.
    All men born have wept salt tears,
    All have wished to run from pain
    And yet to live; all might learn
    To love the sharp maternal brine
    Could salt water taste like wine.

And if we say that we were foreordained,
All that expense of stars was planned
To bring self-consciousness to birth—
Megalomania? Well, we share our earth
With cousins vile enough, clever enough
To make us humble as regards our skill.
And yet, if spiders abash man's pride of life,
They make his charity seem more marvellous still.

    No cost of stars could seem too great
    To have made man's love: love pays for all.
    Harder to think it pays the debt
    For man's pain, man's fall.
    A woman bears a child, and sees
    His doom (her gift) to suffer years

Of hopeless struggle with disease.
Another must endure the cries
Of hunger, with no crumb to give.
And here the radiant face of love
Perishes in a deadly radiance
At the hands of brother men
And the impartial brain of science.

The miracles of science are so often
Just what one would not wish; but then,
God's miracle of the universe
On any view seems worse.
That one should say 'All shall be well'
Is yet the strongest miracle of all.

The flesh that formed us can divide
To form a cancer, and the strength
That held our weakness be dissolved.
Even she, whose affable wit denied
The inordinate, when she came to die
Endured rebellion in her body.
I cannot forget her dreadful sickness,
Nor reconcile within my mind
Her cheerful life, her cruel end.
Yet in her dying eyes I saw
Bright pain and love inseparable,
Part of the truth and ineluctable.

Gide, who forswore belief in God,
Died like a hero, keen to know
The truth of death, and tell it somehow.
Honour to him who rejects nothing,
Peace to all memories! for we too
Would work that miracle if we could:
To taste the truth, and find it good.

Sick Boy

Illness falls like a cloud upon
   My little frisking son:
He lies like a plant under a blight
   Dulling the bright leaf-skin.
Our culture falls away, the play
   That apes, and grows, a man,
Falters, and like the wounded or
   Sick animal, his kin,
He curls to shelter the flame of life
   And lies close in his den.

Children in patient suffering
   Are sadder to see than men
Because more humble and more bewildered:
   What words can there explain
Why all pleasures have lost their savour,
   Or promise health again?
Kindness speaks from a far mountain—
   Cannot touch their pain.

Beecham Concert

A lifetime goes to make this music.
The old body, bundle of bones
Wired together, barely flickers:
Least gestures, costliest pains—
And the sound burns alive from the stick.

Cellini hurled in table, chair,
All that would burn, to cast his metal.
The bronze was flawed despite his care.
But the will itself is inflammable here—
This furnace takes the soul for fuel.

So an old man beats time.
When young men beat, we have in mind
The visible world, and love, and fame;
Here nothing is real but sound,
And death is merely the music's end.

Life is a straw bridging a torrent.
Based on a straw the old man stands:
His style, classical; his dress, elegant;
(On either side the gulf is silent)
Darts of lightning in his hands.

Modern Love

In Almost Cinderella, *the author said,* '*he had wanted to re-create for adults the impact the story had upon children* . . . *Prince Charming* . . . *begins to strangle Cinderella in a very stylised way as the clock strikes. It is part of the mockery of the cliché of love at first sight.*'

See The Times, *7 December 1966*

That strong god whose touch made Dante tremble,
  Who made the sun rise and the stars fall,
    And could make saints of you and me for an hour,
    Now that the world is wise has lost his power:
  He was only a pantomime uncle after all.

'Love for another is simply the willing of good'[1]—
  True for the Middle Ages, a genuine thrill,
    But now such childish fancies are outgrown.
    This is the truth for modern, adult man:
  'Love is simply the perfect wish to kill.'

[1] Aquinas

14

Three Sonnets

In Memoriam the Composer R.H.M.

I

I write no requiem, since rest you have
　　After much torment; nor to compose a dirge,
Since death was your desire; but to bring alive
　　These husky thoughts of you, as on a page
The seedling notes can quicken like the corn.
　　Could I but speak you into life, so long
As the poem lasts, as I can hear reborn
　　The passion which you planted in a song!

If poetry were music . . . but too dense
　　Words seem for this, toneless, durationless.
　　　　Unvalued the visions that a word can raise,
Unvalued the summer leaves and fruits of sense,
　　Beside the sound, so thrilling, sad, concise,
　　　　Of the robin's song on icy leafless days.

II

And myths are true: for wounded against a thorn
　　You made your music. Why you should suffer so,
Being innocent, is more than myths discern,
　　That help us, not to understand, but know.
Innocent, gentle, tormented, gay,
　　The cause of joy in others—such was your nature.
Troubles that can be spoken do not slay;
　　Therefore, till music failed, you could endure.

Lily-field freshets and bells of a Dorset valley,
  Blue lias and gold-capped cliff—O where, where
Is the resignation that we found in Hardy?
    Wild music of wood and heath that made endurable
    The griefs of man, and made that sorrow noble
  Which seems in life an unredeemed despair.

III

To Justice on his calm impregnable peak
  Our cries hurl, our loss, our accusation:
That this should be the inheritance of the meek,
  To die self-tortured, in self-condemnation;
That music is no saviour to its maker;
  That the cause of joy in others finds no cause
To prompt his own rejoicing, and no succour
  Against the rack and flame of his own laws.

Reborn in a song . . . Our clamour dies away;
  The peak of Justice is unmoved and whole.
    Who shall measure a life's loss and gain?
Nothing atones. Only, through the skeleton tree
  A star looks, as an inextinguishable soul
    In the suffering body, irrelevant its pain.

Corneal Graft

And after fifty years of blindness
The hand of science touched him, and he saw.

A face was a blur, poised on a stalk of speech;
Colour meant simply red; all planes were flat,
Except where memory, taught by his learnèd fingers,
Spoke to his 'prentice sight.
                                    As for the moon,
The Queen of heaven, she was a watery curd
Spilt on his window-pane,
For height, more than his stick could measure,
Was a senseless word.
The splendours of the morning gave no pleasure,
But he would rise at dawn to see
Distant cars and lorries, moving divinely
Across his strange horizon, stranger by far
Than the Pacific to the old explorers.

And is the patient grateful, subject of a miracle?

Blind, he was confident, forging through his twilight,
Heedless of dangers he had never seen.
As a dreamer on the brink of a ravine
Walks fearlessly, but waking, totters and falls,
So now the surging traffic appals him,
Monsters menace, he dare not cross:
A child, long past the childhood season;
A prince in darkness, but in the light a prisoner.

And if, after this five-sense living,
The hand of God should touch us to eternal light—
Not saints, well practised in that mode of seeing,
But grown-up babies, with a world to unlearn,

Menaced by marvels, how should we fare?
Dense, slow of response, only at the fingertips
Keeping some fragments of truth—
What could that heaven bring us but despair?

Mirror Image

When I look in the glass
    What creature looks back?
Not myself as I was,
    As I am, as I feel;
That face is not mine,
    Though reason declares
Soul and body are one.
    While my body was ageing
    What was I doing?
While cheeks grew hollow,
    While skin was coarsening,
    Eyelids drooping
    Where was I looking?

I looked at my friends
    And at you, my darling:
As a player who glances
Over his shoulder
    At Grandmother's Steps,
I knew you grown older
    Yet noticed no movement.
In you I engage
    The past and the present
In one bright image
    For ever true.

But while I watched *you*
    The girl in the mirror
Was making a face.
The self that I knew
    Is in focus no longer.
    'I want you to meet . . .'
My looking-glass says,
    And it shows me a stranger.

A Teacher's Funeral

You are present here:
Not *then*, not *elsewhere*,
But *here*, as we kneel, each seeing the same face,
Though inwardly, behind the eyes,
Deeper than the ear's echoes:
Five hundred insights of a single grace.

Single, but variously rich,
As differing in the share of each,
For memory in each has tender things to add;
And each (so confident now) once went
An urchin on those shoulders, bent
To carry children over their terror's flood.

It is no abstract image
That can for a flash our griefs assuage—
This inward touch of a true and loving presence;
As though our pain
Her self could summon
To share our narrow moment and our sense.

If ever earth's pull could make a current
In the heavenly element,
Surely thought so intense must make it stir;
If any pulse of finite love
Beats in the being that spirits have,
Our pulse beats gratitude, beats joy to her.

Thaw

The land takes breath; the iron grip
That clamped upon her heart is slackened.
On roofs the slithering snow-wrack
Like tods of sheep's wool slowly drips.

Earth's grey and foot-patched quilt of snow
Is wearing thin; the green shows through;
The carnival days of ice are gone,
The godlike skater's but a man.

As a sea-bird waddling on webbed feet
He is humbled; see him shamble
Clumsily up the hill, whose nimble
Swoops on the ice were a god in flight.

A curdled gravy chokes the gutters.
Yet on the lake the island glows
In crimson willow-twigs; the trees
Hold up the sky on bare, dark shoulders.

A Waving Hand

'. . . the need to reconcile the fact of what has occurred with
the human imagination of it, to build up a sense of the past
which is also a sense of the present . . .'
                    John Bayley on Pasternak and Tolstoy

The death that we shall die
Is here, we know, coiled like a spring inside us,
Waiting its time.
When what is now becomes the past, we can see its future implied
As seed in the fruit, child in the womb.
The gardener, stooping down to tie
His bootlace, died so,
And acts through a lifetime multiplied
Foreshadowed this: when as a boy
He learnt to tie a bow,
Or when he stooped each day to dibble his plants,
Something was meant, he could not know.

So men seem walking histories
Of their own futures: we look to see the design
Forward or backward, plain,
As rings in a tree-trunk tell the sequence of years.
The jilted boy in pain
Trudging the pavement under the heartless stars
Now with his darling joyfully walks the same street.
Old words, old phrases, fly homing into the future
Where the poem is complete.

Parting a week ago,
The baby waved, through tears. I waved back lightly
With no foreboding fears;
But I remember it now,
And scan and search the memory, as though it should explain

All that came after, the anguish of last night,
The ambulance dash, the kind indifferent nurses,
And now the cot, where she lies in a hospital gown
And waves to me, through tears.

Suppose, when we are dead,
The soul moves back, over the gulf of nescience,
To relive a lifetime, all that was done and said . . .
Some say remorse impels it, the pitiless conscience
That drives toward expiation;
But it might be a different need:
To live each *now* in the illumination
Of what's to come; wholly to understand
Those tears, that waving hand.

Winter Poem

November smells of rue, bitter and musky,
Of mould, and fungus, and fog at the blue dusk.
The Church repents, and the trees, scattering their riches,
Stand up in bare bones.
But already the green buds sharpen for the first spring day,
Red embers glow on the twigs of the pyrus japonica,
And clematis awns, those burnished curly wigs,
Feather for the seeds' flight.

Stark Advent songs, the busy fungus of decay—
They are works of darkness that prepare the light,
And soon the candid frost lays bare all secrets.

A Pirated Edition

Acquaintances
May meet and pass with a brief Good-day,
Yet each takes with him as he walks away
The other's image, lasting on like echoes,
Lingering like the print upon the retina
Of colour and shadow after the eyes close.

Phantoms criss-cross
Are sent from brain to brain, and none
Can call his straying image back again.
What part of me do you carry with you, friend?
Scraps of my speech, flashes of face and form
Unknown to me, that frolic through your mind.

And none can guess
How queerly he haunts another's dream;
How comic or how monstrous he may seem:
Royal personage prancing in cowboy dress
Or unjust judge—a pirated edition
Of his true self, and there is no redress.

'I Want, I Want'

Her body racked, her features crumpled
  Into a mask of woe—
This is Karen, two years old, forbidden
  Some trivial thing, I hardly know
  And she in an hour forgets what grieved her so.

Yet such intensity of sorrow!
  And the childless man who kneels
By his dead bitch, and babbling tries
  To call her back with desperate appeals,
  Who am I, to belittle what he feels?

Absurd to think all sorrows equal,
  And rate the grief of Lear
In the light of eternity no more than these.
  Yet these display what least and greatest share:
  The innocence, the sharpness of desire.

At Coole Park

'The woods at Coole . . . when I am dead . . . will have,
I am persuaded, my longest visit.'
W. B. Yeats: *Autobiographies*

The lady of the house is gone,
And nothing is left of it now, not a stick or a stone.
Contractors crumbled the heart away,
Leaving the rest to its vegetable decay.
And where the word was chief
There runs a wordless riot of stem and leaf.
Yet still the long enclosing wall
Held by the mothering ivy cannot fall;
And in the garden
Are widow's weeds, husks of life like a snake's skin:
Yellow-whiskered Rose of Sharon,
Traveller's Joy, Catalpa Tree,
And Box Walk
That leads to the Copper Beech, her visitor's book,
Where Yeats once set his mark;
Now scribbled over by Tom and Dick and Paddy.

Stranger, here pause,
And do not think to add your name to theirs.
You cannot buy immortality so.
But bend your soul to the touch of terror, know
At the sudden rushing sound
Of wings toward the lake that this is haunted ground.
Pray for this poet who spoke much,
And then beneath the scribbled Copper Beech
Sound the depth of silence,
Noblest monument for such a prince.

Too Much Skill

'*When the artless Doctor sees*
No one hope, but of his Fees . . .
When his Potion and his Pill,
His, or none, or little skill
Meet for nothing but to kill,
Sweet Spirit, comfort me.'
Herrick: *His Litanie*

Weeping relations in a ring
Round the Victorian death-bed stand:
A public, but a gracious ending,
Custom-propped on either hand.

Death with the faithful butler waits
Just farther off, until the soul
Nods an agreement to the Fates,
Keeping a vestige of control,

The end accepted like the start.
Yes, even howls and funeral pyre
Assign to Death his ritual part;
Only our age must play the liar,

Forcing the worn-out heart to hop,
The senile to renew his breath,
Deploying every skill, to reap
A few poor months of life-in-death.

Grant me an artless doctor, Lord,
Unapt with syringe, mask, or knife,
Who when my worn-out body's dead
Will fail to bring me back to life.

Islands of Scilly

For David and Alice Pennant

Dropping like gods from a cloudy sky
Into the jonquil fields the tourists come;
Then, with their sensible shoes, their County drawl,
Scatter as baby spiders out of a cocoon
And melt into the landscape. All
Hunt for the sun, and lay up gold in memory
From recollected daffodils, a hoard
Whose wealth alone plants people on these islands.

Circled by barren skerries, gushers of spray,
Breakers chafing its borders,
Here Tresco lays to heart a calm lagoon:
A tropic in a northern sea,
Where palm joins gorse, and the skin-deep-fertile land
Is pierced through with the jangling tones of ice-plants;
Stone garden in green waters,
With a comb of dark pines and skirt of dazzling sand.

A clutch of islands, every one distinct.
Yet these are fingers thrust to the sky
From a single fist at seven fathoms down;
And so our luckiest days
Rise from the dull, drowned mass of being
In brilliant peaks of joy.

Crab Signals

The Fiddler Crab waves an enormous claw:
   Tumescent signal of desire or hate,
   A summons and a threat.

This locked in battle is like an encumbered knight,
   Who by his heavy armour held immobile
   Can neither retreat nor kill.

The claw has a little, busy, tireless partner
   That forages round for eatable stuff, and then
   Hurries to scrape the monster clean

Of other lives that, given half a chance,
   Spreading like squatters on the passive surface
   Would settle and increase.

Scooping and scouring, it plays a Cinderella part,
   Wholly efficient to its purpose,
   And less absurd, for all its fuss

Than that monstrosity with the signals crossed,
   Or modern men who, bored with tenderness,
   Would bite as soon as kiss,

Would have all lovers raise the equivocal
   Claw-like banner of the aggressive will
   To capture and to kill.

Azalea in the House

This little shabby tree, forgotten all summer,
And crouched in its corner through December frost,
Now is brought indoors to keep its promise.
It speaks in a blaze, like a prophet returned from the wilderness:
The buds throw off their brown extinguishers, burst
Into flame, and March sees a midsummer feast.

Explosion of sunsets, archangels on a needle-point,
Red parliament of butterflies . . .
I cannot hold it with words, yet summer life
While winter howls out there behind the glass
And trees still clench their fists, must be too brief.

Scentless, infertile, kept from moth and rain,
Colour is its whole theme,
Like those vermilion rose-trees that bloom
In picture-books. They never drooped or faded,
But this has only a short month to shine,
And hours not spent in watching it are wasted.

Reading the News

Why does the story always turn out badly?
  In Bluebeard's castle now no rescuer
Comes to redeem the lost, no tears of pity
  Falling from heaven can melt the prison bar.

All these years we have watched the statesmen talking,
  The hopeful signing letters to *The Times*,
And while we dragged our feet, the road was leading
  To famine, torture camps, and atom bombs.

Heroes like Fisher, Grigorenko, face
  The worst of tyranny, while we fast bound
As in a nightmare cannot move a pace,
  And shout for help, but cannot make a sound.

Yet all art is not tragedy, and music
  Cries of a haven, over the storm swell.
Where did they find their faith, the serene masters,
  Their crazy word, that all shall yet be well?

Delphi

Finches in the Castalian stream
Wink a golden wing;
And the deep cleft, where steam
Could spiral into prophecy,
Contains a trickle of water and no mystery:
All the temples are open to the sky.

Arguing over the oracle
Tourists try to eat the plane tree's fruit,
Or choosing picture postcards try
To trap a moment's ecstasy.
All the temples are open to the sky.

Whatever stirred the Delphic seer,
Whether a god's whisper
Or fumes of cyanide as some declare,
No longer speaks. Mycenae is still red,
But with the poppies' blood.
Something remains yet to be understood,

Yet to be reconciled:
The lucid sculpture and the riddling darkness.

Our knowledge and our ignorance
Are brought to judgement here
Between the shining rocks and in the mountain's trance.
Blue the air and bright the stream
Where goldfinch fly;
Dark as ever the god's reply,
Though all the temples are open to the sky.

'Into the Whirlwind'

A documentary, suggested by
Eugenia Ginzburg's book

Here the peaceful flocks are grazing
   Over the green hill;
Lovers lie on a curly fleece;
   Wind wails and is still.
Now the sirens wail, and cease.
Europe trembles, but the siren
   Only called in fun.

And here the nightmare dread comes true:
   Torn from the fireside, whirled
Into the storm, to meet no more,
   Husband, lover, child,
In cell or camp, year upon year,
Now prove how Soviet tyranny
   Outdoes the cruel Tsar.

Those were the 'thirties. Growing in England knew
The common injocundities, the common
Tremors of adolescence, with its fear
To be found out, found wanting, never to be loved.
Surrounding us were the workless, mortified,
Shaming our youthful dilettante distress,
As now her chronicle of torment shames me.
All of us fearing war . . .
               Fears were not liars,
For the day came when the sirens wailed in earnest;
Terror broke from the sky, as we knew it must.
A world ended.
           And a world survived.

Now, as men creep from their holes, what hope
Lifts a faint arc, where the political prisoners
Toil from dark to dark, the deadlong day?
They live in the habitual present tense of pain:
Hope were a span too long to measure, only
Endurance counts, to survive until day ends;
To move, not fall; to live, for a crust of bread.
Life here is a stain in the snow from rag-bound feet,
A wisp of breath, faint as the Arctic sun
Too weak to rise, that lies low on the horizon.
How should the prisoner raise
Her heavy heart, whose only comfort is
That 'each day dies with sleep'?

But gentle sleep's a traitor too,
    For sleep renews the cells
To life, and another day's endurance,
    Though the heart rebels
Against its own absurd resilience.
Brothers, under the same sky,
    They suffer; we go free.

For here again the flocks are grazing
    Over the green hill.
What if the Nazi monster died?
    The heirs of Tolstoy still
Must stain the snow with liberal blood.
And still our lovers' peaceful scene
    Is cross-cut with their pain.

Some Time After

Where are the poems gone, of our first days ?
  Locked on the page
Where we for ever learn our first embrace.
  Love come of age
Takes words as said, but never takes for granted
  His holy luck, his pledge
That what is truly loved is truly known.
  Now in that knowledge
Love unillusioned is not love disenchanted.

The Departure

Words For Music

The Departure, a one-act opera
for two characters with music
by Elizabeth Maconchy, was given
a Sunday evening performance at
Sadlers Wells by the New Opera
Company, conducted by Brian Priestman.

Julia is sitting at the dressing-table in the bedroom, hurriedly making up her face.

JULIA: I shall never be ready in time.
Why, when one specially wants to hurry
Does everything choose to vanish?
My thoughts are all in a snarl,
My fingers are all thumbs.

How *plain* you look, poor girl!
Mark doesn't like me to rouge my cheeks,
But to-day I must, a little,
And now the rouge has vanished.
O, someone has hidden everything—
Nothing is where it should be.
Who would think that this is my own bedroom?
I feel like a stranger—a stranger even to myself.

(The sound of voices chanting, and drawing nearer, is heard. It is a funeral procession. She moves to look out of the window.)

May his soul find peace, whoever he was!
Whoever he *was*? . . . I talk like a pagan:
Whoever he *is*, whoever he may become,
Weightless beyond the burning margin of our air,
A stranger to us and to our ways of feeling
As I—yes—as I feel myself a stranger.

(She turns back.)

Even the room looks strange:
The bed—why is the bed not made?
Wasn't I here last night?
Clouds come rolling through my brain
And all my life seems hidden.
But Mark—I know he is coming,
And I must not keep him waiting.

Mark—O blessed, blessed name,
My frolic joy, my peace.
When he comes, it is May Day:
I shall be free, I shall be gay—
O let him not delay:
Return, return, my love!

But why is this? How strange it is—
I cannot see his face!
I cannot bring his face to mind.
You have been gone too long,
Return, return, my love!

(*Footsteps and voices outside. She goes to the window again.*)

You are coming, beloved. I had your face by heart,
But my eyes failed me. Now I see it with my eyes,
I see your face. And all these are our friends:
Why am I watching, not *with* you?
Here I am! Mark, look up, I am here!
He takes no notice. Mark! Can't you hear me?
Mark! It's useless, I can't make him look up.
He is shaking hands with them all. But what has happened?

(*She turns from the window.*)

Why are we not together?
He looked like a stranger. Someone looked through his eyes
Who would not smile if we met, someone
I do not know—someone I fear to know.
I wish we were safe in one another's arms
Housed in our love, and grief outside, like rain
That falls, and dies in the earth, gone like the dirge
I heard just now.

(*The door opens and Mark enters.*)

You are here at last, my darling!

(*She goes to meet him, but he walks straight past her and
kneels by the bed, his head buried in his arms.*)

A stranger, I said. You have my husband's form,
His walk, his look—ah, but not wholly his look . . .
Lift your head; let me see your eyes again.
Are you deaf and blind? Why don't you answer?
I thought we had been lovers once,
Had lain here together. Lift your head—
Turn, as once you turned in the Square garden
That lies like a green lake in the arid city,
Green in the tundra of the city streets.
Everything stopped for a moment—you remember?—
As though the policeman's hand, checking the traffic,
Waved it to silence, waved the birds to silence,
The spluttering engines and the clattering wren
All stopped as you turned to look,
And I walked on, till under the double cherry
As under nodding Venus, we met.

(*He lifts his head.*)

MARK: Julia! Are you trying to speak to me,
    Or is it my longing that calls your voice from the air,
    Sounding as when we met, under the cherry? . . .

JULIA: 'Good afternoon,' I said, 'What a lovely day!'

MARK (*turning to her*): Julia!

JULIA: Unmerciful God—
    I remember it now, in a flash: the car, the crash . . .
    I died in that crash.
    The stranger who looks from behind your eyes, it is Death!

MARK: Death? I saw you, dead,
    Just now we laid your body in the grave,
    Yet here you stand, exactly as I have longed to see you,
    Have longed to embrace you . . .

JULIA: No, never again.
    I was waiting for you; I did not know that I was dead.
    Where is that Death they paint, with the grinning skull

And gaping eyeholes? I should have recognized him there,
But how could I know him in you? They have not met
  Death
Who paint him like a monster:
He comes with the face that we love most.

BOTH: O, why did we go to drive that day?
Why did we choose that road,
And reach the spot, just at that moment?

O time, turn back, turn back,
Turn back to a safe day
Before the menacing morning,
And bar the door that leads to the dangerous road.

O time, turn back, turn back,
Turn back to a safe day:
Let us start on a different way,
And travel together the lime-flower lanes of peace.

JULIA: But no, it is I who must start, and travel without you;
It is I who must go.

MARK: Don't leave me!
Wait, Julia, remember our life together:
Remember the Summer Ball . . .

Your thistledown dress
That flew with the clock,
That tossed on the music
Like balls on a fountain;
The brilliant wine
Like stars on the tongue.

Our eyes full of love,
Our speech full of nonsense
With bubbles of nonsense
Like air in champagne,
And all the wide halls
Quite empty of pain . . .

JULIA: Long over, the Ball.

MARK: But our child lives still!
He lives; he needs you. For his sake, stay.

JULIA: I see him for ever:
His cradle set by a waterfall,
Wrapped in his shawl,
Our new-minted boy
On the green lawn of the mint-fresh river;
Hands that twirl as the river whirls,
Wordless speech like the gentle jargoning water.
I see him for ever!
But the river, not I,
Must sing his lullaby.
O, life is good, it is hard, hard to leave it.

MARK: Then do not leave it. Stay with me!

JULIA: You hold me back, yet it is you have taught me
What I must do, dear Mark.
Before you came
I only knew that I was not ready,
Hastily rouging my face, combing my hair—
Why was I getting ready?
O, not for you and your most sweet return:
It was my death that I was not prepared for.
We do not recognize death, coming so suddenly,
And we must know our death,
Or else our souls are imprisoned in the past.

MARK: Then, if the past will hold you near me,
So let it be. I'll share your prison,
We'll live in our past for ever.

JULIA: No, dearest, our joy has left those towers
And climbed before us; we must follow.
Joy is afar, over the Alps of loss.

(*The funeral music is heard again.*)

Hark, do you hear that?
Twice he has called me: now I begin to be ready,
I begin to understand his words.
He is saying 'Part. Depart.'
O, Death is our parting,
Nothing else, and so he wears your face for me.
He is saying 'Part, Depart.
You have to depart alone,
And if to meet again,
That does not now concern you.'

MARK: But I hear nothing! Not a voice, not a word.
Where are you going? Do not leave me,
What shall I be without you?
A ghost chirping among the shadows.

JULIA: I am already far:
I am not now what once I was.
Your face is no longer yours.
The being behind your eyes
Is neither enemy nor friend.
Behind your eyes is nothing now
But a bridge, over a black abyss,
A bridge, leading to darkness.
That bridge I cross.

MARK: Joy is afar, over the Alps of loss.
Julia, I am losing you!
Julia, I cannot see you!

JULIA: Nor sight, nor touch, only the word Depart.
Depart. Depart.